MR WOLF'S NURSERY TIME

By Colin & Jacqui Hawkins

EGMONT

${A}$t nine o'clock Mr Wolf set off for a ride on his bicycle. Outside Elsie Marley's house he met three hungry little pigs, who hadn't had any breakfast.

It seems that . . .

Elsie Marley is grown so fine,
She won't get up to feed the swine,
But lies in bed till eight or nine,
And surely she does take her time.

Mr Wolf tried very hard to wake
Elsie up. But she just slept on and on.

By ten o'clock Mr Wolf had still not woken Elsie up. So he went off to Mother Hubbard's Café to have breakfast.

Mr Wolf was hungry and licked his lips as he thought of fried eggs, tomatoes, baked beans, mushrooms, buttered crumpets, sticky jam on toast, a big glass of orange juice and a pot of tea.

However . . .

Old Mother Hubbard
Went to her cupboard,
To fetch her poor dog a bone.

But . . . when she got there
The cupboard was bare
And the little dog gave a groan.

And so did Mr Wolf!

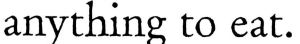

$\large{A}$t eleven o'clock Old Mother Hubbard's cupboard was *still* empty.

And so was Mr Wolf's tummy! So he went around the corner to see whether Little Jack Horner had anything to eat.

When Mr Wolf got there . . .

Little Jack Horner
Sat in the corner, eating a great big pie;
He stuck in his thumb,
And pulled out a plum,
And said, "What a good boy am I!"

And Mr Wolf, who really liked plum
pie, thought so too!

At twelve o'clock
full of plum pie,
Mr Wolf helped
Humpty Dumpty on to a wall.

Nearly there Humpty, just one more push.

How eggciting. Thank you, Mr Wolf.

Unfortunately, when . . .

Humpty Dumpty sat on a wall,
Humpty Dumpty had a great fall.
All the King's horses,
And all the King's men,
Couldn't put Humpty together again!

But Mr Wolf
could – with
some sticky
tape and string.

At nearly one o'clock, after putting Humpty together again, Mr Wolf went to Hickory Dock Station. There he met three blind mice, who said, "What's the time, Mr Wolf?"

Tick tock, tick tock went the station clock. And then . . .

Hickory, dickory, dock,
The mouse ran up the clock.
The clock struck one,
The mouse ran down,
Hickory, dickory, dock!

And Mr Wolf said,
"It's time I got going!"

15

At two o'clock Mr Wolf tripped up and broke his shoe.

So he hobbled back into town and went to the shoe mender.

Cobbler, Cobbler mend my shoe,
Get it done by half past two;
Stitch it up and stitch it down,
Then I'll give you half a crown.

Mr Wolf was so pleased with his
mended shoe that he gave
Mr Cobbler three
silver shillings!

At three o'clock,

on his way back from the cobbler, Mr Wolf got very lost and met Bo-Peep. Bo-Peep said she had left her sheep alone for three minutes. And now they were nowhere to be seen!

Little Bo-Peep has lost her sheep,
and doesn't know where to find them;
Leave them alone,
and they'll come home,
Bringing their tails behind them.

Mr Wolf thought that was a good idea,
as he couldn't find them either.

At four o'clock
it got really hot.
Mr Wolf was thirsty!
So he huffed and puffed
up Wishing Well Hill
to get a drink.

He gave Jack and Jill a BIG fright. BOO!

Jack and Jill went up the hill,
To fetch a pail of water.
Jack fell down
And broke his crown,
And Jill came tumbling after.

But Mr Wolf knew what to do . . .

At five o'clock,

after helping Jack mend his head with vinegar and brown paper, Mr Wolf was hungry again.

So he got his fishing rod and went to catch a fish for his supper . . .

One, two, three, four, five,
Once I caught a fish alive,
Six, seven, eight, nine, ten,
Then I let it go again.
Why did you let it go?
Because it bit my finger so.
Which finger did it bite?
This little finger on my right!

So Mr Wolf decided not to have a fish supper after all.

At **six o'clock,** on his way home, Mr Wolf was very lucky and found a silver sixpence. So he went to have supper at the Palace Restaurant with the King.

They both ate pie and sang . . .

Sing a song of sixpence,
A pocket full of rye;
Four-and-twenty blackbirds,
Baked in a pie.
When the pie was opened,
The birds began to sing;
Wasn't that a dainty dish
To set before the King?

"That WAS a dainty dish," said Mr Wolf.
"Very dainty indeed," agreed the King.

At seven o'clock it began to rain. Mr Wolf was getting very wet when he met Doctor Foster, who had just been to visit Polly the maid. Polly had just been pecked on her nose by a big blackbird . . .

Then . . .

Doctor Foster went to Gloucester
In a shower of rain;
He stepped in a puddle,
Right up to his middle
And never went there again.

Mr Wolf thought that
was really, really funny.

At eight o'clock
the rain stopped, and out
came the moon and the stars.
Mr Wolf saw a dog, a cat, a dish
with a spoon, and a jumping cow!

Hey diddle diddle,
The cat and the fiddle,
The cow jumped over the moon;
The little dog laughed to see such sport.
And the dish ran away with the spoon.

29

At nine o'clock Mr Wolf said
good night, and
a very short time
later he climbed up
the hill to Bedfordshire.

I am...
so...so...sleepy...

Then down
Sheet Lane
to Blanket Fair.

Niddledy, Noddledy, to and fro.
Tired and sleepy to bed we go.
Jump into bed and switch off the light,
Head on the pillow, shut . . . your eyes . . .
Tight . . . shh . . . good . . . night.

Night, night, Mr Wolf!

First published in 2005 by Egmont Books Ltd

239 Kensington High Street London W8 6SA

Copyright © Colin and Jacqui Hawkins 2005

Colin and Jacqui Hawkins have asserted their moral rights

Hardback   ISBN 1 4052 1101 6

Paperback   ISBN 1 4052 1975 0

A CIP catalogue record for this title
is available from the British Library

Printed in Malaysia

1 3 5 7 9 10 8 6 4 2

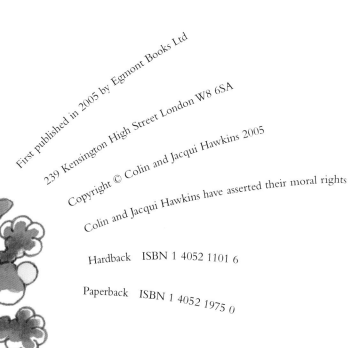

For Sally
From Colin and Jacqui